STERLING

 Keen!

 WARP DRIVE!

 #1

 BANG UP JOB!

 Nicely Done!

 GOOD QUALITY WORK!

 GREAT!

 BERRY GOOD

 A #1

 GOAL!

 Wow!

 AF271801

 ON LINE!

 OOKIE

 HIGH FIVE!

 RECORD BREAKER!

 TOADALLY AWESOME!

 T-REXCELLENT!

 ON TRACK 1234

 YOU'RE GREAT!

 KOALATY WORK!

 PURR-FECT!

 Good Stuff

 Grand

 Major Award!

 KEEP TRUCKIN'

 GO TEAM!

 FANTASTIC!

 WOW!

 THUMBS UP!

Help the duck get to her ducklings.

1

Help the monkey get to the bananas.

Help the rabbit get to her babies.

Help the bear get to his cave.

4

©School Zone Publishing Company 02749

1 one

Find **1** .

✏️ Draw **1** ☀️.

🖍️ Color the picture.

2 :: two

Find **2** 🦋.

Draw **2** ☀.

Color the picture.

3 three

Find **3** 🪰.

Draw **3** ⬭.

Color the picture.

4 four

Find **4** 🍬.

✏️ Draw **4** ⭕.

🖍️ Color the picture.

5 five

Find **5** .

Draw **5** .

Color the picture.

9

6 six

Find **6** penguins.

Draw **6** ✳.

Color the picture.

10

7 seven

Find 7 🦄.

Draw 7 🐟.

Color the picture.

8 eight

Find **8** 🍎 .

✏️ Draw **8** 🍃 .

🖍️ Color the picture.

12

9 nine

Find **9** 🌟.

✏️ Draw **9** ⛵.

🖍️ Color the picture.

10 ten

Find **10** .

Draw **10** .

Color the picture.

Circle the pictures that have the same beginning sound.

 Circle the pictures that have the same beginning sound.

  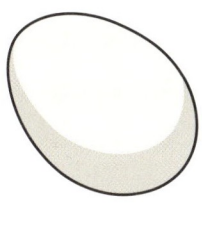

Circle the pictures that have the same beginning sound.

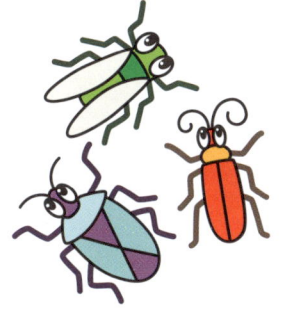  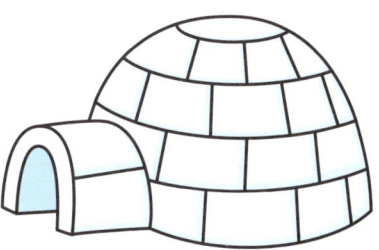

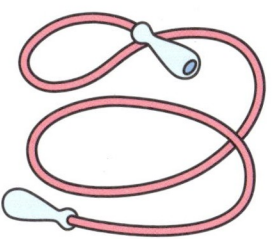 Circle the pictures that have the same beginning sound.

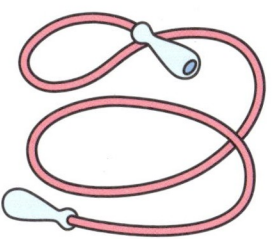

Circle the pictures that have the same beginning sound.

 Circle the pictures that have the same beginning sound.

Circle the pictures that have the same beginning sound.

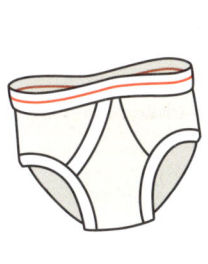

Circle the pictures that have the same beginning sound.

Circle the pictures that **end** with **x**.

Circle the pictures that have the same beginning sound.

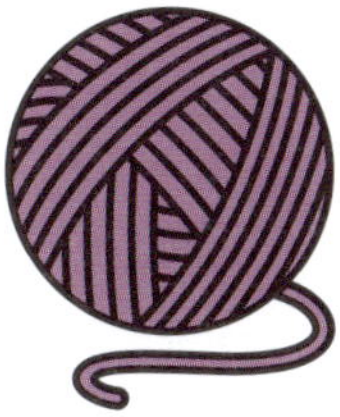

Help the zebra get to the zoo.

23

 Draw lines between the pictures that **rhyme**.

cat

bee

dog

hat

tree

frog

fox

box

24

Draw lines between the pictures that **rhyme**.

rug

bug

sled

mouse

snake

cake

house

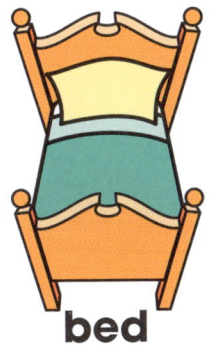

bed

25

Draw lines to match the **opposites**.

on

back

up

off

in

down

front

out

26

 Draw lines to match the **opposites**.

cold

old

new

sad

happy

fast

slow

hot

 Circle the **2** that are the **same**.

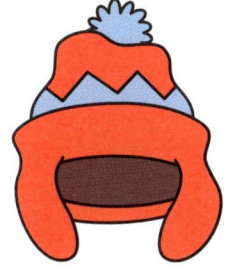  

Circle the **2** that are the **same**.

29

Draw lines between the clowns that are the **same size**.

Circle the picture that is **different**.

Circle the picture that is **different**.

32

Circle the picture that **belongs** with the first one.

Draw lines between the pictures that **belong** together.

chicken

colt

pig

calf

cow

chicks

horse

piglet

Circle the things that **do not belong** in the picture.

Circle the things that **do not belong** in the picture.

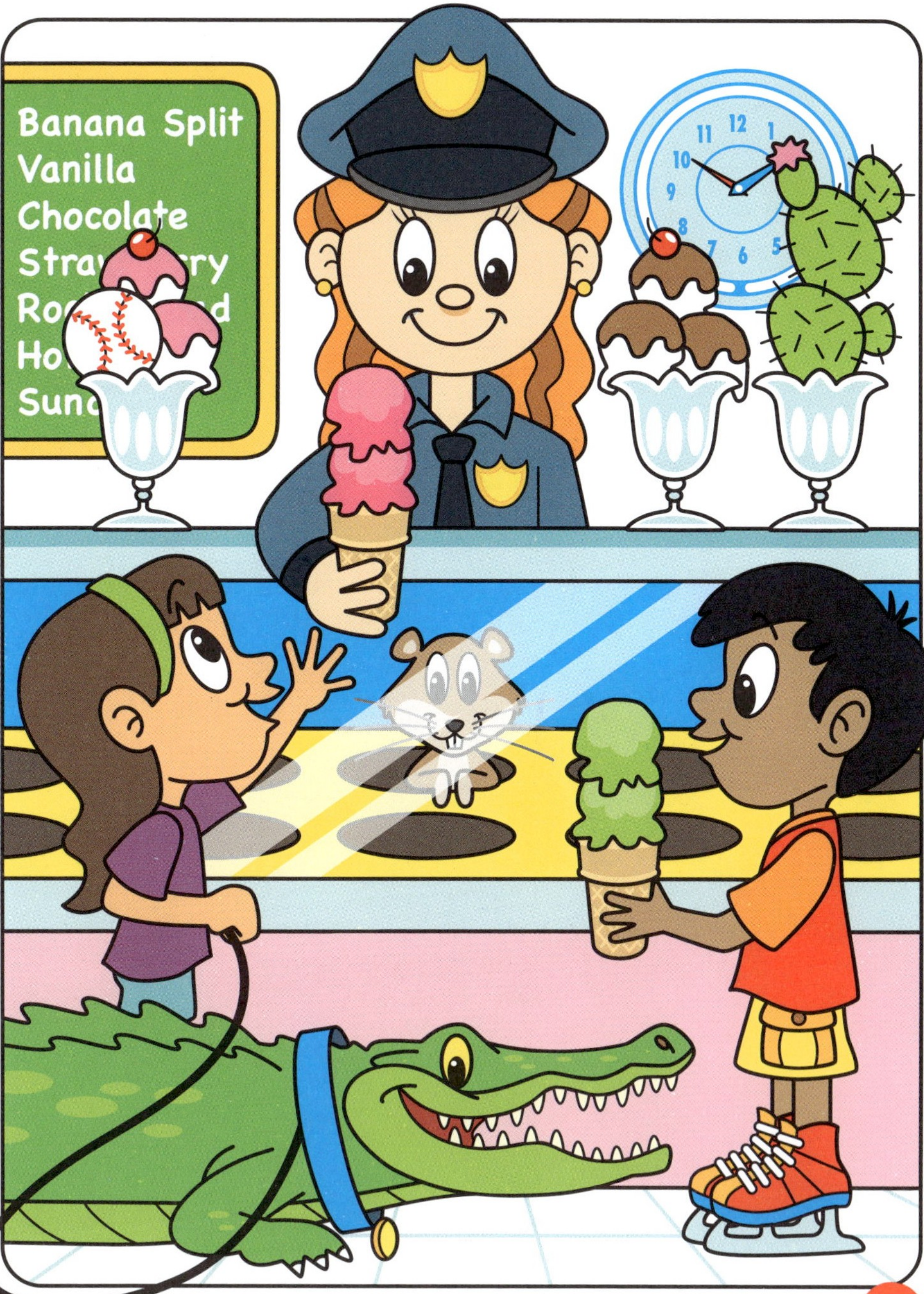
Banana Split
Vanilla
Chocolate
Straw rry
Ro d
Ho
Sund
11 12 1
10
9
8
7 6 5

Color the picture.

1 = red   **2** = yellow   **3** = green

Color the picture.

A = blue   B = orange   C = purple

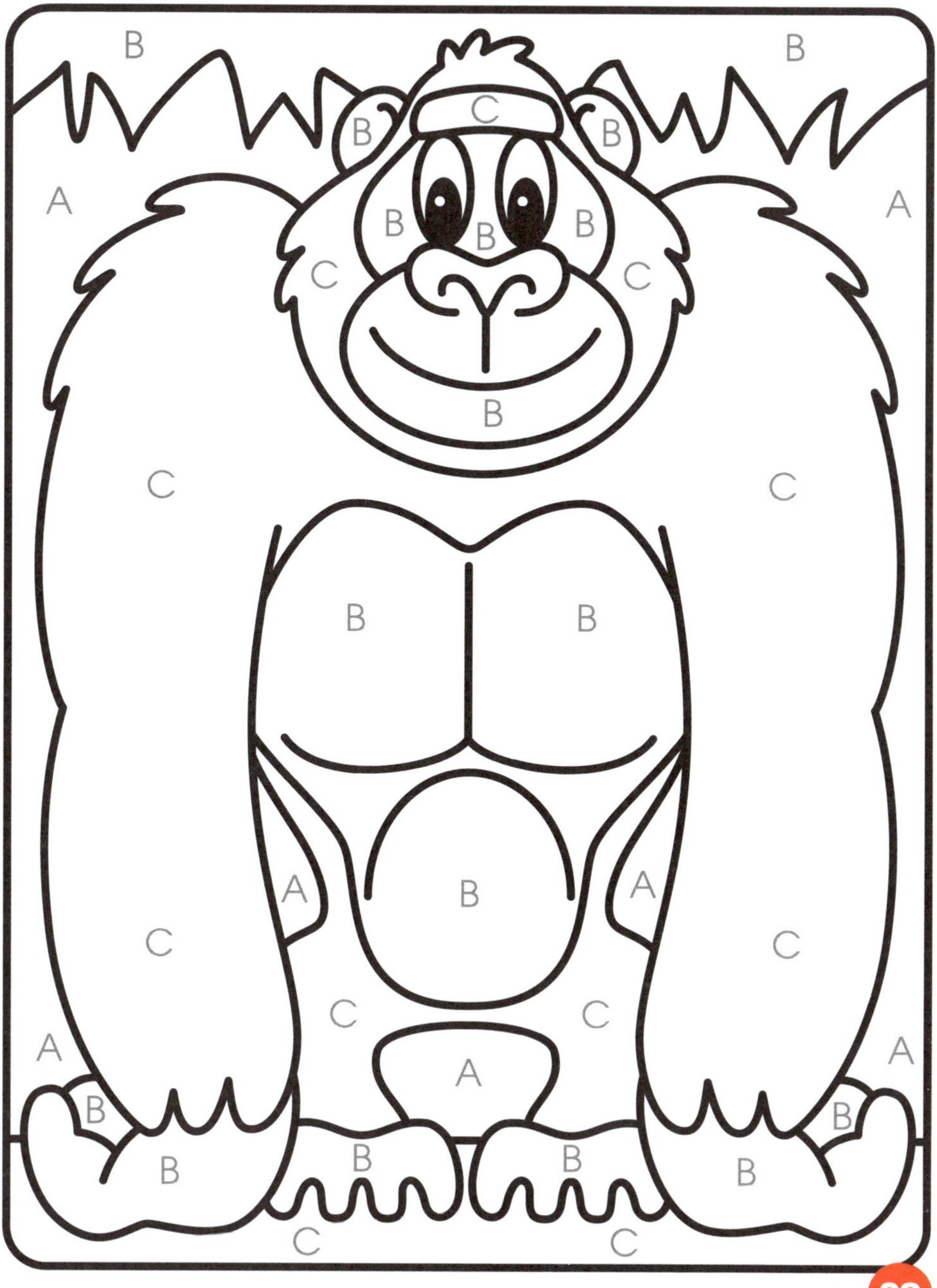

Draw lines from the shapes to the matching pictures.

triangle

square

circle

rectangle

Circle what comes **next** in the pattern.

Circle what comes **next** in the pattern.

Draw what comes **next** in the pattern.

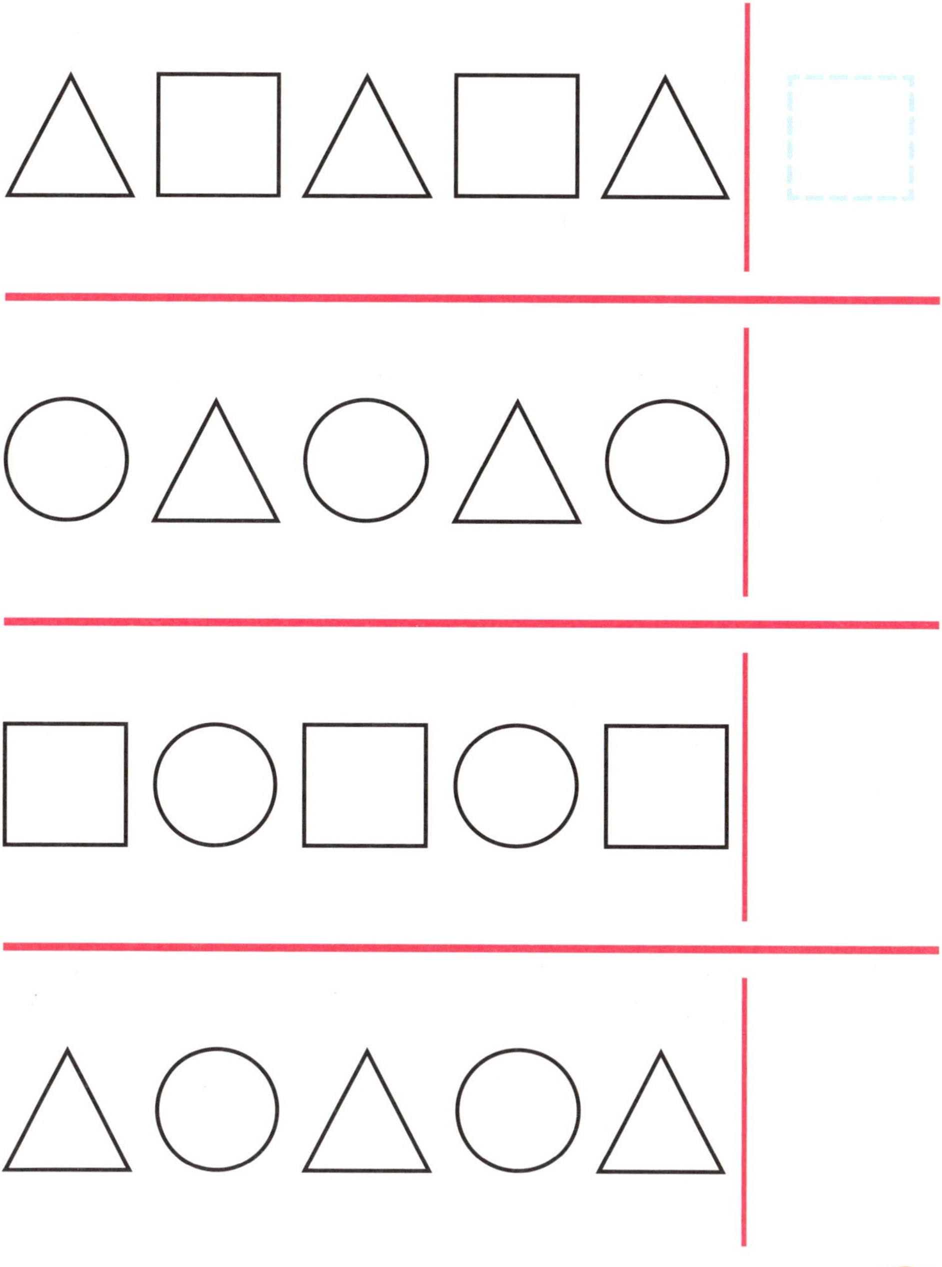

△ □ △ △ □ △

○ △ ○ ○ △ ○

□ ○ □ □ ○ □

△ ○ ○ △ ○ ○ △

Find and circle the pictures.

flower bird fire hydrant cat plant

43

Draw lines to match the children to the weather for which they are dressed.

44

Circle the emotion that matches each picture.

Circle the picture that is **bigger**.

 Circle the picture that is **smaller**.

Circle **10** things that grow on trees.